Jake
our Hero

For Harry
With lots and lots of love
Grandma xxx

CATNIP BOOKS
Published by Catnip Publishing Ltd
14 Greville Street
London EC1N 8SB

This edition first published 2010
1 3 5 7 9 10 8 6 4 2

Text copyright © Annette Butterworth 2009
Illustrations copyright © Nick Butterworth 2009

The moral rights of the author and illustrator have been asserted

A CIP catalogue record for this book is available from the British Library

ISBN 978-1-846471-09-4
Printed in China

www.catnippublishing.co.uk

Jake
our Hero

Written by Annette Butterworth
Illustrated by Nick Butterworth

Chapter One

Jake was excited. It was Christmas!

Jake loved Christmas time. There were lots of lovely things to eat. Boxes of chocolates would appear around the house. Jake would sneak one or two for himself, when nobody was looking. Delicious! His dinner bowl often had very nice leftovers added to it. He loved turkey, with lots of gravy. The odd roast potato was all right and he quite liked cabbage. Jake didn't like carrots, though. He would suck the gravy off, and then leave them spread all over the floor.

Jake's owners, the Fosters, often had friends and family to stay at Christmas and Jake liked that. Everybody was always in a good mood, and Jake would be given lots of attention and lots of walks. He was usually given a lovely, juicy, giant bone. And, best of all, his friend Sam always came for Christmas dinner.

Sam was an old man who lived alone in a house at the bottom of Jake's garden. Sam took Jake for walks in the local park and, through Jake, Sam had become friends with the Fosters. He and Jake were great friends.

Sometimes it snowed at Christmas time, and Jake liked that a lot. He loved to run through deep snow, showering himself all over with it. He liked to eat it! He chased the animals in the park – they left telltale prints in the snow, so it was easy to follow them.

The most exciting thing of all though, was the Christmas party for dogs. Every year, the dog owners who used the park hired the local hall to celebrate Christmas with the dogs. The party usually took place a few days before Christmas day. The hall would be decorated with a Christmas tree and lights. The dogs would arrive, all having been bathed and looking their best. Jake thought that was the only drawback to the party. He hated the bath, but he didn't mind the twinkling bow tie that Mrs Foster tied round his neck.

The dogs had fun together. There were ball games and eating games. There was a race to see which dogs could eat a trail of sausages the fastest. Jake's favourite game was a treasure hunt. He nearly always found most of the treats that had been carefully hidden around the hall. He was so good at it that Mrs Thirkettle had threatened to ban him from taking part, or at least make him wait a while until the other dogs had had a chance to look.

Towards the end of the party, the dog owners had a Christmas meal whilst the dogs had their food together. It was always a very happy time.

Jake couldn't wait to get to the park to see his friends. It was Christmas. And Jake was very excited.

Chapter Two

S am arrived to collect Jake for their walk to the park. He looked very worried.

"Whatever is the matter, Sam?" Mrs Foster asked. "What's happened?"

"You haven't heard the news?" Sam replied. "Holly has disappeared from Emily Thirkettle's garden. Emily went to call her in for the night, and she wasn't there."

Mrs Foster looked puzzled. "That's not like Holly, to escape and run away."

Sam frowned. "Emily says she thinks she has been stolen. Dognapped. She heard Jake barking but unfortunately, she didn't think to see if anything was wrong."

"That's terrible!" Mrs Foster cried.

Holly was the beautiful collie that lived next door. She was Jake's favourite dog friend.

Suddenly Jake remembered something that had happened the night before. He had just finished eating his supper and, as he strolled into the garden, he heard angry voices next door. Jake barked loudly. He didn't like the sound of the voices. As he reached the fence between the two gardens, he heard car doors slamming shut. Then he heard a car screeching away from outside Holly's house. To Jake's surprise and disappointment, Holly wasn't in her garden. Jake had felt puzzled.

"I heard them last night!" Jake thought. "I heard them stealing Holly! I wish I had done something to stop them. Where can they have taken her?"

Jake was very worried.

When Sam and Jake reached the park, the owners of the other dogs didn't make Jake feel any better. Jake listened intently as Sam chatted with Mr Grant. Mr Grant owned Charles, the Irish wolfhound, another of Jake's friends.

"I don't like it one bit," said Mr Grant. "Did you know, Sam, that Mac the Westie has gone missing now? I wouldn't be surprised if they tried to steal Charles. Mrs Thirkettle lives only two doors away from me. I will have to be extra careful. I'm very glad we are going away tomorrow. We'll be back in time for Christmas. I hope they catch the thieves before then."

Sam looked very concerned. "Yes, let's hope the police can find out what is happening, and soon. I would hate it if Jake was stolen."

"Oh, you don't need to worry about Jake, Sam. He isn't a pedigree dog. These thieves seem to know what they are after and have only stolen valuable dogs. They can probably get plenty of money for dogs like Holly and Mac. I have heard of several other pedigree dogs that seem to have disappeared in suspicious circumstances as well." Mr Grant paused and looked at Jake. "But no mongrels. Of course," he continued, "if they did steal a mongrel by mistake, they would probably get rid of it, dump it pretty quickly."

Sam was livid. "Jake may not be a pedigree, but he is the most precious thing in the world to me, and I can't bear the thought of him, or any other dog, being stolen, or 'got rid of'! What a dreadful thought!" Sam said angrily.

"I was only trying to cheer you up, Sam," said Mr Grant.

"Well you could have been a bit more sensitive

about it," Mrs Thirkettle interrupted. "Can we change the subject please? I have come to the park today for some moral support, instead I am now worried that Holly could be killed! I don't feel very supported!"

Jake felt the same. He didn't know whether to feel pleased that nobody would want to steal him because he wasn't a pedigree, or offended! And it did seem that he was right, that Holly had probably been stolen. She *was* a very beautiful collie.

"At least she won't end up being dumped." Jake thought.

He shivered. To end up lost and far away from home seemed a terrible thing to happen to a dog. But, even worse, to be killed. Surely that couldn't happen. Could it?

"And what about Mac?" Jake thought. "He's not here either. Has he been stolen as well? This is awful!"

Mac was a West Highland white terrier and another of Jake's friends. Jake liked him a lot. He was older than Jake, but he still loved playing with a football and they had some good games together.

Jake felt very gloomy. "I might never see either of them again!" he thought.

This was such a sad thought that his excitement about Christmas vanished. The

Christmas party would be an awful time.

"Things just aren't the same without friends," Jake thought, miserably.

Jake plodded round for the rest of the walk, showing no interest in the ball when Sam kicked it for him.

"Poor old fellow," Sam said to him, "you know something isn't right, don't you? Come on, let's take you home."

That night, Jake lay awake, worrying about his friends. If they were in the hands of a gang of thieves, what might happen to them? Surely nobody would want to hurt the lovely Holly! Jake thought this seemed so cruel. Didn't these thieves have hearts at all? Didn't they care that these dogs were precious friends and companions?

Chapter Three

The next day brought more bad news.

"Morning, Sam," Mrs Foster greeted Sam as he arrived at her house to collect Jake. "Isn't this a terrible business about Holly? Emily Thirkettle received a ransom note this morning. It was pushed through her door on a scrappy piece of paper. The thieves want five thousand pounds! She's called in the police."

Jake listened carefully. So it was true. Holly *had* been stolen.

"She is in danger," Jake thought, "and there's nothing I can do!"

"Oh, then my worst fears are confirmed!" said Sam. "This is awful. We will need to be sure that nothing happens to Jake."

Sam and Jake made their way to the park, but Jake walked very slowly, with none of his usual bounce. Sam tried to cheer him up by playing football with him, but Jake wasn't interested. Eventually, Sam gave up and took Jake home.

When the pair arrived back, Mrs Thirkettle was sitting with Mrs Foster, and she seemed very agitated.

Mrs Foster greeted Sam and Jake.

"You weren't gone very long, Sam? Are you all right?" she asked.

"Yes, I'm OK, thank you Susan, but it's Jake here. He didn't want to play. I think he is missing Holly," Sam replied.

Mrs Foster looked at Mrs Thirkettle.

"Emily was just telling me more disturbing news. Apparently, the police have details of another dog, a bloodhound. His owners have received a similar ransom note to Holly's. It seems there is a gang stealing the dogs. And it's true, they are threatening to do away with the dogs if their ransom demands are not met!"

"I don't know how I am going to raise five thousand pounds for their ransom!" cried Mrs Thirkettle.

"No, and you shouldn't Emily. The police have said that you mustn't give in," Mrs Foster said.

"Well, if I had the money, I would pay it. I would give anything to have Holly back," replied Mrs Thirkettle. She looked desperate.

Sam and Mrs Foster didn't know what to say. They knew just how much Holly meant to Mrs Thirkettle.

"This is such awful timing as well, with Christmas coming. Nobody will feel like celebrating, not until the dogs are home safe and sound," Mrs Foster said.

"The police believe that is the reason so many dogs have gone missing now. The thieves are able to sell the pedigree dogs on for huge sums at Christmas time," Mrs Thirkettle said, sadly.

Jake now felt even worse than when he was in the park. He felt angry that anyone could do such a thing. Dogs were being stolen, for

ransom. Holly was locked up somewhere, maybe being badly treated, so that her owner would pay money to get her back. It sounded like Mrs Thirkettle didn't have the money, so what would happen?

"The trouble is," continued Mrs Thirkettle, "that the police are so busy at the moment, that they don't seem to have the time to look for the dogs. I don't know what to do," she said, in despair.

Mrs Foster and Sam looked at one another.

"Well, let's have a think," said Mrs Foster. "Perhaps we should try to find the dogs ourselves. We could start by printing some posters with photographs of the dogs. We could stick them up around the town. People could look out for the stolen dogs, report anything suspicious, that sort of thing. We could try to make folk aware that their dogs are in danger."

"Perhaps we should get in touch with the other

owners whose dogs have been stolen. It always helps to work together in times like this," Sam said. "It helps to know that you're not alone."

Mrs Thirkettle was very grateful. "It sounds like a very good idea."

Jake listened as they discussed their plans and wondered how he could help. He desperately wanted to find his friends but he didn't know how.

Jake spent the rest of the day moping around the house. He didn't eat his dinner, not even when Mrs Foster mixed some leftover cold beef in his meal.

"Oh, Jake, what are we going to do with you?" Mrs Foster sighed. "You miss Holly, don't you? I just hope we find her soon. If I can't get you to eat, you will end up skin and bone!"

It was time for Jake to check around his garden before bedtime. He wandered around, not really expecting to find much, when suddenly, he heard a sound from next door, in Charles's garden. Jake listened carefully. He could hear somebody.

Jake knew that Charles and his owners had gone on holiday that morning, so it wasn't them. Jake was about to bark a warning to Mr and Mrs Foster when he stopped himself.

Jake wanted to get a look before he barked. If he barked now, the intruder might run away. Jake crept closer to the fence and peered through the hedge.

There were two men in Charles's garden. They were both big men, quite tall, and one was very fat. Jake sniffed the air. He could smell the same smell that was in the air the night Holly disappeared. Jake was sure these men were the ones that had taken Holly!

They were looking for something. Jake listened from his hiding place.

"Now listen, Alf. If the dog's not in the garden,

I'm not going to try and nick him from the house. That's burglary," the fat man said.

"I know that, Dick. We'll have to keep out here till they let him out," Alf replied.

"Perhaps we've missed him out here?" Dick pondered.

"Dick, we're looking for a wolfhound, do you know how big they are? Do you think we've fallen over him by mistake? It's only the biggest dog there is, you dope!"

Dick looked hurt.

"I don't know nothing, Alf," Dick mumbled.

"Then let me do the thinking," snapped Alf. "We'll hide in this hedge, until the dog comes out."

The two men backed themselves into the same bush that Jake was hiding in, on the other side of the fence.

Jake was now convinced that these men were the dog thieves.

"I should do something quickly," he thought.

It was a very brave thing that Jake did next. He jumped over the fence into Charles's garden and landed on top of one of the thieves.

"Ughhh what's that?" cried Dick. "It's a wolf!" he said, trying to push Jake off.

Jake pinned Dick to the ground and growled into his face.

Unfortunately for Jake, these men were dog thieves, experienced in dealing with dogs. They had come ready to capture Charles, a much bigger dog than Jake. Before Jake had time to dodge out of the way, Alf threw a big sack over his head. Dick grabbed Jake's legs and bundled the rest of him into the sack. Jake struggled and barked loudly, but the sack muffled his barks. The thieves ran out of the garden, carrying Jake in the sack and threw him into the back of a van, which was parked out in the road. In no time at all, they were speeding away from the

house, and nobody had heard a thing.

"Brilliant!" thought Jake. "Instead of helping to save Holly, I'm going to need saving myself!"

The thieves were almost as fed up as Jake.

"Well that's just great!" Alf exclaimed. "Instead of nicking a valuable pedigree wolfhound, we've ended up with a worthless mutt. What's Sankey gonna say about that?"

"Do we have to take him with us, Alf?" asked Dick. "He's not going to be worth much."

"He'd have barked his head off. Of course we have to take him. Anyway, maybe we'll get a few bob for him." Alf grinned. "You know what Sankey does with some of them, mongrels, or ones the owners won't pay up for."

"Yeah, I know," Dick replied, "but I don't like it."

Jake shivered. He could guess where the unwanted dogs ended up, and he didn't like the idea either. Not one bit!

Chapter Four

As the van sped along, Jake wriggled out of the sack and found himself in a big metal cage. Jake could smell that dogs had been in the van, and one dog in particular: Holly. Jake felt excited.

"Perhaps I'm going to the same place as Holly. I hope so!" he thought. Jake wondered where that might be. He lay down as close to the front of the van as he could and listened to the thieves.

"No, I don't like it, Alf," Dick said. "I don't like the way Sankey treats them. It's horrible!"

"Don't be so stupid, Dick. You shouldn't be nicking them, then. Sankey's right. This is business," Alf replied.

"Why can't we just let them go, if the owners don't pay up? Let them try to find their own way home?" asked Dick.

"You big lump of lard! How long before the police found us then, eh? You shouldn't be doing this job, Alf. You should be working for the RSPCA or something. You're too soft. Let them go? I've never heard such rot, and that's with listening to you all day!" Alf braked hard and Jake was thrown against the side of the cage.

"Be careful, Alf. What did you do that for?

Is he all right?" Dick looked nervously behind him at Jake.

"Never mind that mangy mutt. I nearly missed the lane!" shouted Alf.

The van bumped along a rough track until it came to a stop.

Jake strained to hear what was going on. He could hear voices. The voices were getting louder until Jake could hear three men outside the van. He recognised Alf and Dick but there was a third man with them, and he was angry.

"Well, you better let me see him," the man shouted. "Get him out. Now!"

The van door opened. The thug called Dick opened the cage and grabbed Jake's collar. Jake struggled to get free, but he didn't manage to escape the lead that Dick clipped to his collar.

"Out you come, now, and be a nice boy for me." Dick held Jake by the lead.

Jake was determined not to be a nice boy.

He leapt out of the van before Dick was ready. Dick fell out behind Jake and Jake dragged him along the ground until Alf stepped in and stopped them.

"Oh, I see! An awkward customer, eh? So, instead of bringing me a valuable specimen of a wolfhound, you two have brought me this mutt that looks like a wolf, and a wolf with attitude! Well, easy done I suppose. How big is a wolfhound, did we say? About the size of a small pony. Hard to miss, you'd think. Still, you two managed it! Useless!"

Jake didn't like the look or sound of this new man.

Alf and Dick looked at each other.

"It's his fault, Sankey," Alf shouted. "The dog attacked him and he panicked. I had to rescue him. We had to bring the dog, to shut him up!"

Dick looked hurt and started to protest.

"Enough! I've heard enough. Take him over to the barn. Leave him there, and I'll decide what to do with him," Sankey growled.

"A barn!" Jake thought.

Jake decided to allow the

thieves to lead him to a large barn.

"See!" Dick said. "He can be a good dog. You've just got to handle them right."

"Just shut up!" Alf replied. "You've dropped us right in it, you have. It's going to take a lot to make Sankey calm down. Let's get him in the barn first, before you start crowing about how good you are with dogs."

It was dark inside the barn. Alf unlocked the huge old door and Dick led Jake through the doorway. Dick took the lead off Jake's collar then attached a long rope to it instead.

"Now you stay there, you." Dick said to Jake. "I'll bring you something to eat in the morning. You can lie on that straw. It won't be too bad, you'll see."

"Dick, stop talking to the dog. He can't understand you, you're only going to upset yourself when he goes. You've got to stop making friends with them. This is business," Alf said.

On their way out of the barn, Jake heard the thieves relock the big padlock on the barn door.

"So, that's it. I'm tied up and locked in," Jake thought. "Hard to escape from this place!"

He lay down on the straw and began to wonder if there was anyone else in the barn with him. There hadn't been any noise when the thieves brought him in. It had seemed strangely quiet.

But now he could hear something. Jake listened carefully. There was a sound coming from behind him. Jake peered into the darkness. As he looked, a shaft of moonlight suddenly shone through a crack in the barn door. It illuminated a pile of straw bales. As Jake's eyes got used to the half-light, he thought he could see some very small shapes on top of one of the bales. The shapes had eyes, and the eyes were looking back at him.

Jake could see some very little dogs, puppies perhaps. He barked loudly. He was pleased to see company and said so.

Suddenly, a little dog jumped out of the shadows next to the straw bales, and leapt at Jake, telling him urgently to be quiet.

To Jake's surprise, and pleasure, it was Mac, Mac the Westie.

Mac was pleased to see Jake as well. He explained to Jake that the dogs had agreed that they would not bark, because if they did, the thieves punished all of them, not just the one that barked. If they stayed quiet, the thieves didn't tie them to a rope, like they had Jake. It meant they all had the freedom of the barn.

"All of them?" thought Jake.

Anxiously, Jake asked Mac if he had seen Holly, but before Mac could answer, dogs started to appear from out of the shadows, daring to come out of their hiding places.

It was hard to see in the gloomy barn. There were several shapes coming towards him, but none of them looked like the one he most wanted to see. Perhaps she wasn't here after all. Jake began to feel very disappointed, when he felt a friendly nudge from behind. It was Holly!

They were delighted to see each other. Jake leapt in the air, and then he asked Holly if she was all right. She was, and so happy to see Jake. But their joy at being reunited didn't last long. They both knew they were in a very dangerous situation.

Jake was determined to appear brave, telling

Holly that he would find a way to get them home. Holly knew that Jake meant well, but she also knew that this time, even Jake was going to find it hard to find a way to escape from this awful place.

Soon, there were more dogs crowding round Jake, and Holly introduced him to them all.

Claude was a bloodhound. He had been taken captive some weeks previously. In fact, of all the dogs, he had been in the barn the longest. He was a natural pessimist. He told Jake that he was not a bit surprised that his owners hadn't paid the ransom demanded for him. They were probably glad to see the back of him.

Jake tried to explain that the police had asked the owners not to pay the ransoms and the reason for this, but Claude didn't listen. He was convinced that he would never see his home again.

Whilst Jake was trying to cheer him up, the

tiny puppies pestered Claude, pulling at the
folds of his skin. One of the pups swung in the
air on Claude's long ear and then disappeared
under the huge folds of Claude's skin until Jake
couldn't see him. The puppy was having great
fun, but Claude wasn't enjoying it at all. He
shook himself vigorously, trying to get rid of
the puppy, whilst still talking to Jake. Eventually,
Claude became cross with the puppy, at which
point a little poodle came out of the shadows

to rescue him. It was Peaches, the puppy's mother.

Jake looked at Peaches in astonishment. He had never seen such an unusually coloured dog. Even in the moonlight, Peaches really looked the colour of a peach.

Unfortunately for Peaches, as she explained to Jake, she had been stolen just before the birth of her puppies. They had been born in the barn. Peaches shivered as she remembered that one of the thieves, Alf, had wanted to take the puppies away to drown them. The other thief, Dick, had taken pity on them. Somehow, he persuaded Alf that the puppies would be very valuable.

The puppies were now able to see and crawl, but they were tiny and very vulnerable. To Claude's disgust, the puppies had adopted him as their favourite uncle. They were fascinated by the folds in his skin. They loved to clamber all over him, and were not a bit put off by his gruff moods.

Jake looked at the dogs crowding round him. He felt dismayed. They had all been stolen for their looks. They were very valuable dogs, but they were not strong dogs.

Jake asked Mac if there were any more dogs around the farm. If there were others, hidden somewhere else, they might be able to join forces.

Mac thought the only other dog on the farm was a German Shepherd prowling around in the farmyard. His name was Rex, and the thieves seemed to be using him to guard the dogs in the barn. Rex had come into the barn on a few occasions, when the dogs were fed. Rex was a fierce-looking dog.

Jake asked if any of the dogs had tried to befriend Rex. If he wasn't *very* fierce, maybe Rex could help them. After all, reasoned Jake, he was a dog, and he might want to help.

It hadn't occurred to any of the dogs in the barn that Rex would be anything other than nasty towards them.

Then a gloomy voice made itself heard over the hubbub that was filling the barn. Claude reminded the other dogs that they were making a terrible din and rather than escaping, they would soon be tied up on rope tethers if they didn't shut up. Claude repeated his view that none of the dogs' owners would pay up and they would all end up dead. He added, as he tried to shake one of the puppies off his ear, that he thought the puppies would be first, for being such nuisances.

Peaches shuddered and called the puppies to her.

Jake was determined that this was not going to happen to him. He would try his hardest to escape.

"Tomorrow," he thought, "I'll try to talk to this Rex. See what he has to say."

The dogs settled down for the night, huddled together for warmth on the straw surrounding Jake. Jake's arrival had cheered them up. Somehow they would survive this, they thought, together.

"Let's hope so!" Jake thought. "It would be nice to get home for Christmas!"

Chapter Five

"Welcome to the studio, Mr Haagen. Mr Haagen is here today to tell us about this dreadful business of the stolen dogs," the presenter said.

Sam had been invited along to the local radio station. They were keen to help in the search for the dogs.

"So, Mr Haagen, tell us about the missing

dogs and what can we do to help?" the presenter asked.

"There are posters up all over the town, showing photos of all the missing dogs. Please stop and look at them. If you see or hear anything suspicious, dogs barking where there didn't used to be any perhaps, then please call the police," Sam said anxiously.

"I understand that you have a particular interest in one of the dogs," the presenter said.

"Yes, Jake. He is the best friend I have ever had. He saved my life," Sam said. "He is very precious to me and his owners, Mr and Mrs Foster. We were so shocked when he was stolen. I feel devastated, like I have lost part of me." Sam paused. "All the dogs are important to their owners. There are some very worried people at the moment."

"I can see what this means to you, Mr Haagen. You have our full support," the presenter said.

"So listeners, look out for these dogs, let's find them soon."

When Sam had finished the radio interview, he joined the Fosters and the other dog owners. They were going to hand out leaflets, showing photos of the dogs.

"Right, does everybody know where they are going?" asked Mr Foster.

They were standing outside a big department store in the centre of town, surrounded by a large crowd.

"Has everybody got enough leaflets?" asked Mrs Foster. "We have got plenty. If you run out, just find Sam. He will stay here and make sure everybody knows what they are doing."

The streets were busy with people doing their Christmas shopping, but most people stopped to take a leaflet. Many were horrified to think of what might happen to the dogs if they were not found.

"I can't bear to think of life without Jake," Sam said.

"We'll find him. Don't you worry, Sam. The whole town knows about him now," Mr Foster said. "And knowing Jake, he won't be taking this lying down!"

Mrs Foster smiled. "No, that's true. Knowing Jake, he'll be trying his best to get home. We mustn't give up hope."

"I hope Holly is with Jake. He is such a brave dog, I know he will try to protect her," Mrs Thirkettle said.

"I should think they are all together. The police said they thought it was the same gang who had stolen them all. Let's hope they are all still safe," Mrs Foster said.

"All this publicity can only help. Everybody I have met today heard Sam on the radio. One lady I met said she was moved to tears when she heard how these precious dogs had been stolen," Mr Grant said. "I felt quite guilty when we got home from holiday to find that Jake had been stolen. I miss the rascal. He's such a character."

"We are going to find him. And all the other dogs. We won't stop until we do." Mr Foster was very determined.

Once all the leaflets had been handed out, the volunteers were invited to the Fosters' house for a mince pie and a warming cup of tea.

"I have a question to ask you all," Mrs Foster said, once everybody had his or her cup of tea.

"Do you think we should go ahead with the dogs' Christmas party?"

There followed a long discussion as to whether this would be a good idea or not. It was hard to decide what to do. If the dogs weren't found, what would there be to celebrate?

"Shall I tell you what I think?" Mrs Thirkettle had been quiet until now. "We all know that Christmas is a time to celebrate, to have fun, and to enjoy ourselves. But Christmas is also about hope. Because of that, I think we shouldn't give up hoping that the dogs will be home in time. I think we should go ahead with the party."

Everybody cheered Mrs Thirkettle. It was decided the Christmas party would go ahead, as planned. Meanwhile, everybody would do their best to find the dogs. That would be something really worth celebrating.

ake woke early. Something was tickling his
nose. He opened his eyes to find one of the
puppies licking his face. Its tail was swishing
across his nostrils. Jake sneezed loudly.

The puppy jumped in surprise and rolled off
Jake onto the pile of dogs that were huddled
together around him.

The rest of the dogs stirred in their sleep but
they didn't wake up. Jake decided to get up and
explore as far as the rope would let him. He
stretched himself awake and then found that

the rope would just reach to the barn door. Jake could see it was still quite dark outside.

At the barn door, Jake thought he could hear a noise on the other side. There was a small gap at the bottom of the door and Jake could see a black shadow. Jake pushed his muzzle into the gap as far as he could and tried to see what was making the shadow. He could smell a dog. He guessed it was Rex.

On seeing Jake's muzzle beneath the door, Rex started to move away. Jake called softly to him, asking him to come back. Rex hesitated. Jake called again, telling Rex that he wanted to be friends and that he didn't think it was Rex's fault that he was being made to guard the dogs in the barn. Rex didn't answer, and carried on walking.

Jake was very disappointed. He slumped back onto the straw. Slowly the other dogs woke up. They were as disappointed as Jake when they heard about Rex's response. Jake felt he had to try again. Rex could know something that might help them. If only he could be persuaded to talk to them.

The day wore on, until it was nearly time for the dogs to be fed. Suddenly, Jake could see a dark shadow beneath the barn door. Rex was back.

Quickly Jake stretched towards the door. He introduced himself through the gap and Rex answered him!

Rex was afraid the thieves would be along soon, and they didn't have long to talk. He explained to Jake that he really didn't like having to stand guard over the barn. The thieves had stolen him from his owners and had decided to keep him, rather than dump him. Rex was worried that, if he didn't do a good job of guarding, Sankey and his crew would get rid of him.

Jake sympathised, but explained to Rex that, perhaps, with Rex's help, they could all be rescued.

Rex hoped so. He asked how he could help.

Jake asked one thing. Did Rex know if anyone or anything ever came to the farm regularly?

Rex thought for a while. A postman came every day. He rode a bike. The rubbish lorry came, Rex thought, once a week. Every other day, a milkman called at the farm. He drove an open-sided car-type-thing, a milk van.

Excitedly, Jake asked Rex if he knew when the

milkman was next due to come.

Rex replied that, as the milkman had not called today, he would probably be here tomorrow. He usually called about the middle of the morning.

At that moment, Dick and Alf arrived with the dogs' food.

The puppies were fed first. Dick had prepared some special food for them.

"Come on little ones. Eat all this up, now. You need to build yourselves up, it's getting colder. They say snow is on the way." Dick patted the puppies.

"This is going to end very badly, Dick. You are getting much too fond of these dogs," Alf said.

Once the puppies were satisfied, Dick turned his attention to Jake.

"This new one, Alf. He's been as good as gold. Can I let him off the rope?" asked Dick.

"No, you can't. I don't like the look of him at all. He stays on the rope. That's that." Alf scowled at Jake.

After all the dogs had been fed, Alf left the barn, leaving Dick to clear up.

Dick went to the barn door to check that Alf had gone, and then he went over to Jake.

"Come here, mate," Dick said. "Let's take that off you. You'll be all right without it." Dick undid the rope tether attached to Jake, in defiance of Alf. "I hate to see dogs tied up. There you are."

When Dick had left, Jake rushed around the barn, from one end to the other, so overjoyed to be free of the rope. This was perfect. The puppies joined in, and one of them tripped Jake who landed right on top of Claude.

Claude muttered grumpily, telling them not to mind him, he was just lying there, minding his own business. They must feel quite free to completely flatten him.

Jake apologised to Claude but added that, perhaps, Claude could start to have a little fun himself.

Claude thought it unlikely that he would have much fun if he ended up being dumped by the thieves, but he allowed himself a little smile as he said it.

"He's cheering up a bit!" Jake thought.

Suddenly Mac called out. He was acting as watchdog and he had something to report.

Through a dirty, broken window, Mac could see thick flakes of snow. It was snowing heavily.

All the dogs shivered. Back home, with cosy houses to return to, it was fun to play in the snow. They could get cold and wet and it didn't matter, because they had warm fires to lie in front of and dry beds to sleep in. But stuck here, in this draughty barn, the snow wasn't going to be any fun at all.

Jake shook his head. He wasn't going to stay

in the barn any longer. After talking to Rex, Jake had had an idea. Tomorrow he would try to escape. He wanted to get home in time for the Christmas party, if possible. He told the dogs his idea. They listened carefully.

The puppies then wanted to know about the party, so the dogs settled down on the straw, and Holly and Jake described the fun they had at Christmas with all the dogs from their local park. Jake liked the games best and Holly liked dressing up. They both liked the food but best of all, they agreed, was being together, just having fun.

The dogs went to sleep that night, not knowing what tomorrow might bring.

Jake felt restless. He may have thought of a possible way to escape but would the snow ruin his plan?

Chapter Seven

The next morning, Rex arrived at the barn door, just as it was getting light. He had news for the dogs.

All through the night, the snow had continued to fall, and now everywhere was covered in a blanket of white. The thieves were clearing a way through the snow, so that they could use their van. Rex thought they might be thinking of moving the dogs. They were busy clearing away any evidence of the dogs from the farm. If

Jake was going to escape, it had to be today. Any delay and it might be too late.

Jake checked that all the dogs, including Rex, knew what to do when the time came. Everybody was ready and determined to play their part.

Rex went off to a lookout position. The dogs in the barn waited for the signal. Everybody was silent, even the puppies. All of them listened intently. The milk van must come.

The morning dragged by. The milk van didn't arrive at its usual time, and the dogs waited. Lunchtime came and went and still the milk van had not come. The dogs began to despair.

Dick and Alf came over to the barn with food for the dogs. Jake lay quietly on the straw. He wanted Alf to think he was still tied up.

As Dick and Alf entered the barn, the dogs heard the noise they had all been hoping for. It was Rex, barking very loudly. That was the signal.

Suddenly, the pack of quiet, docile dogs rose up from the straw and rushed around the barn, barking and howling. They charged at Dick and Alf, tripping them over. They then all bundled on top of the thieves.

"Oi! Get off me, uugh! I've got a face full of slobber!" Claude was pinning Alf to the floor, pushing his head into Alf's face.

"Oh, come on you beauties!" Dick said to Holly, Peaches and the puppies. They were all sitting on top of him. "Let me get up now!"

Seizing the opportunity, Jake rushed through the open barn door out into the snowy farmyard.

Making its way, very slowly, up the snowy track was the milk van. Rex was running alongside it, barking.

Jake hid himself in a corner of the farmyard.

As the milkman got out of his van, Rex barked and jumped up at him.

"Goodness, you're noisy this morning, aren't you fellow?" The milkman took some milk out of one of the crates on the float. "What's worrying you? Did you think I wasn't coming? I didn't think I would make it either. Still, here I am."

Whilst Rex distracted the milkman, Jake jumped aboard the van. It was full of milk crates, some empty and some with used bottles in them. The farm was the milkman's last call.

As the milkman got back to the milk van, he looked across at the barn. He could hear the sound of more dogs barking very loudly. He was puzzled. He had never seen any other dogs on this farm apart from the German Shepherd.

The milk van set off back down the track to the lane. Jake tried to find a flat area to lie down on, but the whole of the back of the van was full of crates. Jake stood with two feet inside one crate and his back feet inside another. As the milk van skidded along the icy lane, Jake had great difficulty balancing on the crates. They slid about on the slippery metal surface of the van, which rocked about along the bumpy, snowy lane.

At one point, the van skidded to an abrupt

stop, and Jake was thrown forward into a pile
of crates. He lost his balance and fell off into a
deep drift of snow.

Shaking himself, and trying to make as little
noise as possible, Jake frantically tried to jump
back onto the van but the snow had made the
van very slippery. Jake couldn't find his footing

and his attempts at jumping back on ended with him falling back into the snow. Desperately, Jake tried to jump on again. Again he slipped back into the deep snowdrifts. Then, to Jake's dismay, the milk van started up again. It was driving away, leaving Jake stranded.

"Come on!" Jake told himself. "I have got to get back on that van!"

Jake ran as fast as he could, but the snow was clinging to his fur, making his legs feel heavier with every stride. He watched as the milk van moved further and further away.

Jake began to think that he had lost his chance, but then, the van slowed and stopped, before turning into the main road. Summoning all his strength, Jake leapt after the van. It was now or never.

As the van began to move off again, Jake made one huge last effort. He jumped… and landed noisily amongst the milk crates. Quickly, Jake hid himself as best he could, hoping that the milkman would not look behind.

Fortunately for Jake, the milkman was used to noisy crates rattling around. All his attention was concentrated on the icy road.

Slowly, the milk van made its way into town. At last, the van arrived at the milk depot. Jake waited until the milkman came round to the back of the van before he jumped up, barking.

The milkman was astonished to see him.

"How on earth did you get there?" he said.

Jake's barking had alerted other people in the depot. They came out of the office to see what was going on.

"What have you got there, Len?" a voice called across the depot yard.

"Goodness knows, Brian," Len, the milkman replied, looking at Jake. "Funny though, he looks familiar. Hang on a minute while I go into the office. I need to look at something."

He returned, holding one of the Fosters'
leaflets.

"Look at this, Brian. This was handed to me
the other day. Looks like him, doesn't it?" Len
said, pointing at Jake.

Jake barked loudly.

"How come he's on your van?" Brian asked.

"Well, he wasn't there before my last call. He

must have jumped aboard at the farm. And now I come to think of it, there was a lot of noise going on in the barn there. Dogs barking. Quite a few of them by the sound of it." Len paused. "I think I should call the police." He patted Jake.

"Hurrah!" thought Jake, and leapt about in the snow, jumping for joy.

"He seems to think that's a good idea!" Len laughed. "Right. Let's get you into the office. I expect you could do with some milk. Perhaps we should find you something to eat as well. I'll see if we've got anything. And I'll get onto the police."

A relieved Jake licked the milkman's hand and followed him into the depot office. At last, help would be on its way to the rest of the dogs at the farm.

Chapter Eight

It was late afternoon in the Fosters' house. Mrs Foster and Sam were busy wrapping the last few dog presents in preparation for the dogs' party the following day.

"I am finding it very difficult to summon up any enthusiasm for this party, Sam. I know we said we would go ahead with it, but I had hoped that Jake and the others would be back by now," Mrs Foster sighed.

"I know," Sam replied, glumly. "But we said we would do it, and we can't let the others down."

Mrs Foster agreed.

They carried on wrapping the presents until

there were only two left to do.

Suddenly the telephone rang. Mrs Foster answered it. "Hallo, yes. Yes, that's me. Yes. Really? Are you sure?"

There was a long silence, whilst Mrs Foster listened to the caller. Then she cried, "Oh, that's absolutely wonderful! Yes, yes, I will be there straightaway! Yes, I'll come right now. Bye!!!"

Mrs Foster put the telephone back and let out a loud whooping noise.

"He's back! They've found him!"

Sam hardly dared to believe what she was saying. "Jake? Have they found Jake?"

"Yes, yes, Sam. Jake's been found, on a milk van of all things! That's led the police directly to a farm, and to the rest of the dogs. They were being kept in a barn. All the dogs are at the police station, safe and sound." Mrs Foster was so excited. "They have arrested three men. The police are pretty sure they are the culprits."

Happily, Mrs Foster and Sam rushed to the police station to collect Jake.

"Mrs Foster, is this your dog?" a policeman asked, pointing to Jake.

Before Mrs Foster could answer, Jake bounded past the policeman, and threw himself at Mrs Foster and Sam.

The policeman laughed. "You don't need to answer that! You have a remarkable dog there. It's thanks to him that we found the farm and the other dogs. We can put a stop to this nasty business once and for all, now we have the culprits locked up."

The owners of the other missing dogs arrived just after Sam and Mrs Foster. There were lots of happy reunions. The police had even been able to find Rex's owners. Rex jumped for joy.

Mrs Thirkettle was very tearful. Mac's owners were delighted. All the dogs were extremely excited. Even Claude was overjoyed to be reunited with his owners. Peaches' owners were thrilled to see her and her puppies. They seemed so healthy. They wondered why.

"Two of the thieves seem hard nuts, but a third one, Dick, I think his name is, has been very helpful. Bit of a softie, I think. He seems to have fed the dogs quite well. He asked after the escaped dog, he was worried about him. He meant your dog, Mrs Foster, Jake. It might help Dick's case, when it comes to trial," the police officer said.

When everybody had calmed down a bit, Mrs Foster had something to say.

"You must all come to the Christmas party tomorrow. It will be a lovely time, now that all the dogs are safe." She paused. "I think the Christmas baths will be just in time, they all smell of the farm!"

"This is the best Christmas present I could have wished for!" Sam said, hugging Jake.

And Jake had to agree!

Chapter Nine

Jake was so glad to be home that, for the first time in his life, he didn't mind having a bath. He allowed Mrs Foster to wash and dry him without once making a fuss. Mrs Foster was amazed. After she had brushed him, she put a black bow tie round his neck. It had little coloured lights on it that lit up when a button was pressed.

"Don't you look smart?!" Mrs Foster stood back to admire Jake. "It's lovely to have you home." She hugged Jake tightly. "Let's go and find Sam. We mustn't be late for the party."

All the other dogs and their owners were at the hall when Sam, Jake and the Fosters arrived. To Jake's surprise, the dogs and their owners formed a guard of honour for Jake. As he walked down the middle of the two lines of dogs, the owners clapped and the dogs barked. Thanks to Jake, the dogs had been rescued. Everybody was very happy.

The party was a very special time. Jake loved it. He won most of the games that involved eating. He especially liked the sausage trail, but Claude the bloodhound sniffed out a lot of the pieces of sausage before Jake. They both shared the pieces they found with the others. Claude even chewed one tough piece a little to soften it for Peaches' puppies.

"Claude's going to miss those pups!" Jake thought.

Holly was declared the best-dressed dog. Mrs Thirkettle beamed as she was given Holly's prizes. There was a new collar for Holly and a box of chocolates for Mrs Thirkettle.

After the party games, the dogs were served their food. As Jake shared a big bowl of meat with Rex, he thanked Rex for his part in their escape. Rex tried to say it was nothing, but Jake knew differently. Without Rex, the whole plan would have failed.

There was still one more surprise. When the dogs had finished eating, the owners sat down for their party meal and the milkman, Len, arrived in time to join them. The dogs rushed to greet him, and Jake licked his face.

"It's lovely to see you again, Jake. My, don't you look smart!" Len said.

"We're so glad you could come," Mrs Foster

said. "We've saved you a place. Come and sit down here. You are most welcome."

At the end of their meal, Mr Grant stood up.

"Attention everybody. I would like to propose a toast," Mr Grant said. "Have you all got your glasses ready?"

Everybody raised their glasses.

"A toast," continued Mr Grant, "to Jake. The bravest, boldest dog I know. To Jake." Then he looked around. "Where is he?" he asked.

Everybody looked. Nobody could see Jake.

Then Sam spotted a tail poking out from beneath a tablecloth. He walked over to the table and raised the cloth. There, heartily tucking into Mrs Thirkettle's box of chocolates, was Jake!

Everybody laughed, and chorused together, "Oh Jake!"

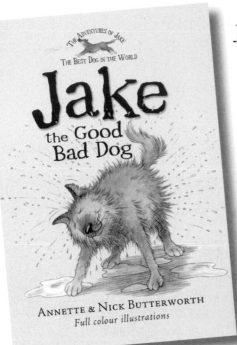

Jake loves to chase ducks, dig up the roses and play with dirty washing. Can his dream of going to Crufts, the best dog show in the world, really come true?

When injured birds are found in the park, the finger points at Jake. Jake knows he's innocent but can he prove who the real culprit is?

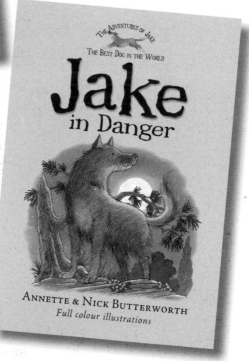

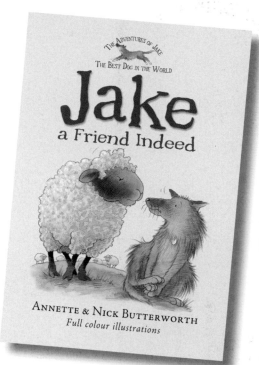

The Adventures of Jake
The Best Dog in the World

Jake
a Friend Indeed

ANNETTE & NICK BUTTERWORTH
Full colour illustrations

It's exciting being on a farm, but Jake can't help getting into trouble. How can he show everyone that he's not just a stupid town dog?

Jake's favourite park is under threat. The council want to sell the land for building. It's time for Jake and his friends to get into action!

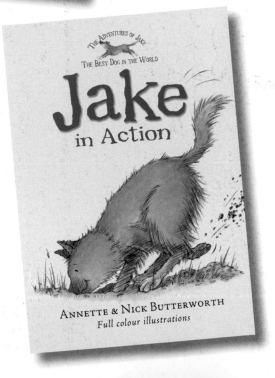

The Adventures of Jake
The Best Dog in the World

Jake
in Action

ANNETTE & NICK BUTTERWORTH
Full colour illustrations